Uncle Kawaiola's Dream

A HAWAIIAN STORY

by

Victor C. Pellegrino

illustrated by

Linda Rowell Stevens

Uncle Kawaiola's Dream: A Hawaiian Story, Victor C. Pellegrino
Copyright © 2010 by Maui arThoughts Company
All Rights Reserved.
Illustrated by Linda Rowell Stevens
Editors: Shelley J. Pellegrino and David B. Merchant
Hawaiian Language Consultant: Hōkūao Pellegrino
Hawaiian-English Reference: Pukui, Mary Kawena and Elbert, Samuel H. *Hawaiian Dictionary: Hawaiian-English, English-Hawaiian.*
Honolulu: University of Hawai‘i Press, 1971.
Art Photography: Steve Brinkman
Printing Consultant: Rizwan Awan
Printing: AMICA International, Kent, WA
Printed in the Republic of Korea: 05/15/2010

Library of Congress Catalog Number: 2009920403
Publisher's Cataloging-In-Publication Data
(Prepared by The Donohue Group, Inc.)

Pellegrino, Victor C.
   Uncle Kawaiola's dream : a Hawaiian story / by Victor C. Pellegrino ; illustrated by Linda Rowell Stevens.

   p. : ill. ; cm.

 ISBN-13: 978-0-945045-08-3
 ISBN-10: 0-945045-08-5

1. Maui (Hawaii)—Juvenile fiction. 2. Maui (Hawaii)—History—Juvenile fiction. 3. Taro—Planting—Hawaii—Maui—Juvenile fiction.
4. Maui (Hawaii)—Social life and customs—Juvenile fiction. 5. Maui (Hawaii)—Fiction. 6. Historical fiction. I. Stevens, Linda Rowell.
II. Title.

Published by
Maui arThoughts Company
P.O. Box 967, Wailuku, HI, USA 96793-0967
Phone or Fax: 808-244-0156
Phone or Fax Orders: 800-403-3472
E-mail: booksmaui@hawaii.rr.com
Web Site: www.booksmaui.com

DEDICATION

To my children
Laʻelaʻeokalā, Mahinamālamalama, and Hōkūao

To my grandchildren
Kamehanaokalā and Kaʻimi

To my wife
Wallette Pualani Lyn-fah

To my parents
Adeline and Albert Pellegrino

and

To all the kalo farmers and people helping to restore the ʻāina

INTRODUCTION

Restoring loʻi on the island of Maui and throughout the state of Hawaiʻi is a dream shared by a small but growing number of passionate, dedicated, and hard-working people. They may or may not be ethnically Hawaiian. Kalo just has to be "in their blood." This is the foundation for *Uncle Kawaiola's Dream: A Hawaiian Story*—the story about a young man who possessed a passion about Hawaiian culture and particularly loʻi kalo restoration and kalo cultivation.

Uncle Kawaiola's Dream: A Hawaiian Story is a simple story about the fulfillment of a young Hawaiian's dream. The narrative is set in Waikapū, Maui, where in 1848 about 1,800 loʻi were in full production. In fact, Nā Wai ʻEhā—Central Maui's four major streams of Waikapū, Wailuku, Waiehu, and Waiheʻe—provided water for what was then the largest contiguous kalo-growing region in all of ancient Hawaiʻi. The story, which is historical fiction, is about one of those ancient loʻi being restored by a community of people.

Uncle Kawaiola's Dream: A Hawaiian Story also highlights the importance of storytelling in Hawaiian history and culture as a means to perpetuate Hawaiian cultural traditions and values from generation to generation. By telling his niece and nephew his special dream story about how family and friends came together to restore a loʻi, Uncle Kawaiola passes on to the next generation the significance of certain basic Hawaiian cultural values such as laulima, kōkua, ʻohana, and kuleana. By telling the children about his opportunity to return the ʻāina for its intended use—agriculture—he reinforces the connections between the ʻāina and the wai that Hawaiians respect.

Uncle Kawaiola's Dream: A Hawaiian Story can be read for enjoyment or used as a springboard to motivate children as well as adults to pursue similar dreams. Perhaps the experience of a loʻi restoration recorded in this story will inspire present and future generations to restore the ʻāina in other areas of Maui and the state of Hawaiʻi.

After reading the story, some may want to learn more about kalo, the basic staple of the Hawaiian people for many hundreds of years. For example, there is much to be learned about how the Hawaiians faced enormous destruction of their loʻi by sugar plantations and developers. When the sugar companies leveled many kuleana lands containing loʻi kalo and diverted the stream water from Nā Wai ʻEhā to irrigate their fields, Hawaiians had to leave their land because they could no longer farm wetland kalo.

To help readers expand their knowledge about Hawaiian culture, traditions, and history, I have included *A Study Guide for Understanding and Learning* at the end of the book. A *Glossary* is also provided as a reference for those who are unfamiliar with the Hawaiian language, geography, and ethnobotany. It also includes words found in the *Introduction* and *Afterward*.

Finally, I hope everyone enjoys the story and the wonderful illustrations by artist Linda Rowell Stevens.

Victor C. Pellegrino
Waikapū, Maui, Hawaiʻi
2010

Uncle Kawaiola's Dream

A Hawaiian Story

Uncle Kawaiola, Hoʻāla, and Naupaka sat on the bank of a loʻi next to a kīpapa stone wall.

"Please tell us the story about your dream, Uncle Kawaiola—the one about how the ʻāina came back to life," asked Hoʻāla.

Naupaka nodded her head in agreement. "Yes, Uncle. Tell us the one about our kalo farm."

There were many stories Uncle Kawaiola enjoyed sharing. He especially liked telling the one about his dream. And he especially liked telling it to children.

His eyes shifted toward the quivering kalo leaves in the loʻi. He thought about his great grandfather Nahau who once planted kalo there. He also thought about the day when he first saw the water flowing back into his family's ʻāina.

Then he took a deep breath and launched into his story. It was a story so many knew and called "Uncle Kawaiola's Dream." It was a story that inspired many who heard him tell it.

"This story began a long, long time ago. It started before we were even born."

Uncle Kawaiola's eyes shifted once again toward the quivering kalo leaves in the loʻi.

Hoʻāla and Naupaka were all ears. "Uncle," asked Naupaka, "how could you have had a dream before you were born?"

But he didn't answer her. Instead, he went right on with his story, almost as if he were living the dream he was telling.

"Our kūpuna lived on this ʻāina more than 150 years ago. They farmed kalo here just like their ʻohana had done for hundreds of years before that."

"Hō," said Naupaka. "That sure was a long time ago."

"Go on with the story, Uncle," said Hoʻāla, anxious to learn more about his kūpuna.

"One of those kalo farmers was Nahau, who was my great grandfather and your great-great grandfather." Kawaiola looked up at the blue sky dotted with white clouds. "He would be proud if he could see our lo'i now."

Just then Uncle Kawaiola's voice changed. "But something sad happened. Your great-great grandfather Nahau, and many of our kūpuna, were forced to stop growing kalo. They stopped because they didn't have enough water for their lo'i kalo."

"Did it stop raining?" asked Naupaka.

"No, the rain didn't stop," laughed Uncle Kawaiola. "Actually, several large companies began growing sugar cane. Water from our streams was diverted to irrigate their cane fields. Soon, not enough water was left for our kūpuna to grow kalo, and the lo'i dried up. The ground cracked, and invasive weeds and koa haole trees grew all over the lo'i. Eventually, the ancient kīpapa stone walls fell down. Many of our kūpuna had to leave their kalo farms to find work elsewhere because they could no longer live off the 'āina."

"But today we have some water in our streams and ancient 'auwai, Uncle," said Ho'āla. "What happened?"

"Well, sugar cane is not grown much anymore, so now there is a little more water for us to grow kalo again. But a lot of water is still being diverted for other uses, so there's not enough water to restore all of our lo'i."

Uncle Kawaiola pointed mauka from where they were sitting. "You see up there? That's where your great-great grandfather once farmed kalo. Those lo'i are all waiting for more water from our streams."

"But let me tell you what led up to that day when the two of you and many others came to restore our lo'i and return the water to our 'āina," said Uncle Kawaiola.

Naupaka and Ho'āla moved closer to Uncle Kawaiola. They didn't want to miss a word of his story.

"One day a friend from O'ahu came to visit me. His name was Kalima. He knew a lot about growing kalo. He remembered many stories he had heard from his kūpuna.

"Kalima said to me, 'Kawaiola, your land once had many lo'i. Now they are hidden by the trees and grasses. The 'āina is waiting for you to rebuild these lo'i and start growing kalo again.'

"I asked him, 'But how can we bring the 'āina back to life? It is too much work for just my father and me.'

"'Dream it, Kawaiola. Let the Hawaiian in you dream it. But take small steps,' Kalima replied.

"Again he said to me, this time softer, 'Take small steps, Kawaiola.'

"I think he wanted to find out if I was listening with my heart and not just my ears."

Ho'āla added earnestly, "We're listening carefully too."

Then Naupaka moved her feet back and forth. "See, small steps," she said softly.

Ho'āla and Uncle Kawaiola smiled and began laughing. Naupaka laughed too.

"After Kalima returned home, my father and I decided to make a path into our land with our machetes. Our work began with a pule. Then all of a sudden, a pueo soared above our heads."

"What did it mean, Uncle?" asked Naupaka.

"It meant something good," said Ho'āla. "All Hawaiian families have an 'aumakua."

"You're right, Ho'āla. The pueo was telling my father and me something. I think it came to tell us that we were doing the right thing. It was happy to see we were restoring the 'āina to grow kalo."

"Several months passed. My father and I finished clearing some koa haole trees and tall grasses on a small portion of our 'āina. The ancient kīpapa stone walls were beginning to reveal themselves, welcoming the morning sun, bathing in the evening moon, and most of all, waiting to hold the waters that would flow from the ancient 'auwai into the lo'i. But this was only the beginning. There was a lot more work to do.

"I asked my father, 'Why can't we get help from my friend Kalima and our neighbors, friends, and relatives? We can ask kalo farmers on Maui and from the other islands to help us too.'

"I saw my father's face swell with doubt. 'I don't think people do that anymore, Kawaiola,' he said. 'How are you going to get all those people to come here to work, and for nothing? It's not even their 'āina. Besides, everybody today is busy with their own lives.'

"But I insisted, 'Kalima opened his own lo'i. He also helped others restore their lo'i. If he leads us, we can open at least one of our lo'i in just one day, bring in water from the ancient 'auwai, and plant our first huli. He told me we can do it. He said that we just have to take small steps.'"

Ho'āla knew Uncle Kawaiola's father. He wasn't the kind of person who rushed into things, but he always supported his children. Naupaka asked, "Well, Uncle, were you ever able to change your father's mind?"

"Yes, he liked the idea of taking small steps to get things done. I think he was a lot more patient than I was. So we sent letters to friends, family, and kalo farmers to ask for their kōkua. Everyone was excited about helping us restore the lo'i. As for myself, I was so impatient. I couldn't wait for the day we would really begin the restoration."

"But you have a lot of patience now," said Ho'āla.

"That's true, Ho'āla. I learned from my father and Kalima. I think my kūpuna were also trying to tell me something. I am sure they wanted to see if I could do things a little at a time—step by step."

Even though they were all talking about the importance of being patient, Naupaka still couldn't wait for Uncle Kawaiola to go on with the story of his dream. "Then what happened, Uncle? Finish your story," she pleaded.

"The day before work was to begin, Kalima flew in from O'ahu. He brought his family too, and we began planning. Kalima suggested that we start work at six in the morning. 'It is important that we begin soon after the sun rises so that we can work the full day,' he advised.

"The next morning I awoke early. I was eager to begin restoring the lo'i. At that moment, I think that my dream was really beginning."

Naupaka looked puzzled. "You woke up and your dream began? Didn't you have the dream while you were sleeping?" she asked.

"Well, you'll find out, Naupaka. Soon about fifty people gathered at our farm. We made a circle and joined hands for a pule. It was very quiet. The words of the pule echoed across the terraces. The 'āina was listening too. It was waiting to hold the life-giving waters that once nourished the kalo. At nine o'clock that morning, people were still arriving. By noon, more than 120 people were shoveling earth, cutting koa haole trees and hau, pulling stumps, moving stones, and leveling the lo'i. It was a sight to see!"

Uncle Kawaiola's thoughts turned back to that first day. He remembered how everyone had worked together. Then he raised his voice, startling Naupaka and Ho'āla. "We are reclaiming the 'āina. My dream is coming to life. I see the first step right before my very eyes!" he exclaimed.

Naupaka started shuffling her feet. "See, step by step. Kalima told you so."

"Kalima and some workers climbed the sloped land up to the ancient 'auwai. His quick and trained eye soon found the old, worn path where the water once flowed down to the lo'i. Kalima was sure that it was where Kawaiola's great grandfather had brought his water in.

"The crew started clearing the land and digging a ditch for the water. Before long, Kalima broke through the earthen wall of the 'auwai.

"A liquid gold mixture of earth and water began flowing into the ditch from the 'auwai. Slowly it made its way down the 'auwai to the lo'i that had waited so many years to receive its nourishing waters once again.

"As the water entered the lo'i, men and women continued to churn the earth with picks and shovels. Some of the kūpuna tied a rope to each end of a large log. Then the younger men and boys began pulling the log back and forth across the lo'i to level it. Children romped in the muddy water, too young to work, yet still happy to think that in some way they were participating in something important."

"Wasn't I there too, Uncle? I think I remember being all covered in mud," exclaimed Naupaka.

"I remember," said Ho'āla, proud that he was older and could remember the events of that very important day. "That was when you were only a few years old, Naupaka. I remember it well because you and I were covered in mud. We helped Uncle build the mud banks for the lo'i. At the time, I don't think we understood all that was happening on Uncle's 'āina."

"No worry," said Uncle Kawaiola. "Did you know that you two are part of my dream too?"

Naupaka and Ho'āla looked surprised.

Uncle Kawaiola's eyes glistened in the sunlight. His face was all smiles.

"The biggest part of my dream was about planting the first huli. I gathered all of the huli I had prepared for planting. They were ones I had been dry land farming for several years. They were waiting for just this day. I arranged each variety of huli into piles. There were mana 'ele'ele, lehua, and moano 'ula'ula.

"Everyone was anxious to participate in the first planting. Most important to me was the planting of the mana 'ele'ele. You see, this was the kalo I discovered growing in the valley above our 'āina.

"Naupaka and Ho'āla, I don't know if you remember everything that day. But before we began planting, it began to rain. It didn't last long. It was a sign though—one we Hawaiians know well."

"A sign of what?" asked Naupaka.

"Don't you know?" asked Ho'āla. "It means something good. It's a special blessing."

"It was," replied Uncle Kawaiola. Then he became silent for a moment before continuing his story. For Naupaka and Ho'āla, it seemed as if that moment of silence lasted forever. But then he began.

"My mother and father were the first to plant huli," Kawaiola said proudly. "Both of them were happy to be the first to plant. I pushed my handmade 'ō'ō kauila into the soil. Below the water, the earth opened. It was ready to receive its first roots of life. My father turned to me after planting his huli. His face glowed. We didn't need to speak. I knew what he was thinking about—the pule, the pueo, and the rain."

"Did you plant next?" asked Naupaka.

"No. It was more important for our 'ohana to be next. You see, kalo is all about family. The little plants that grow from the mother plant are called 'ohā. That's where we get the Hawaiian word for family—'ohana. We always take care of family before we take care of ourselves."

Naupaka and Ho'āla looked at Uncle Kawaiola as he gazed upon the 'āina. They could see that he was pleased with the restoration. He looked at the dark green kalo leaves quivering in the wind. Just then, a pueo circled overhead before perching on the huge, twisted kukui tree next to the lo'i.

Uncle Kawaiola looked up. The late afternoon sky was turning a soft reddish orange.

Then Uncle Kawaiola whispered softly, "Great grandfather Nahau, we have restored your 'āina. We have brought the lo'i and the ancient 'auwai back together again. We have replanted the huli, and the pueo can now return to its home."

Uncle Kawaiola was pleased. His great grandfather Nahau must have been pleased too.

"And that's the story of my dream," Uncle Kawaiola said, his smiling eyes shining down upon Hoʻāla and Naupaka.

Hoʻāla and Naupaka stared in wonderment at Uncle Kawaiola.

"But the dream came true, Uncle," said Hoʻāla.

Not fully understanding the difference between dreams and reality, Naupaka asked, "If dreams come true, are they really dreams?"

"Dreams can come true if you have passion, if you are willing to work hard to make them come true," Uncle Kawaiola explained. "And of course, you need people to guide you and help you reach your dream, like your parents, your ʻohana, and your friends."

Hoʻāla and Naupaka looked up at Uncle Kawaiola. The corners of his lips formed a gentle smile. His eyes turned once again to the kalo growing in the loʻi.

Then Hoʻāla and Naupaka smiled too.

Hoʻāla whispered softly but firmly into Uncle Kawaiola's ear. "I have a dream, too, Uncle. I'll take it in small steps, just like you."

Naupaka echoed the words of Hoʻāla, and added emphatically, "Me too." Then once again she shuffled her feet back and forth to imitate the idea of taking small steps to get something done.

Uncle Kawaiola touched his nose to Hoʻāla and Naupaka's noses. All three sat silently, watching the sun setting behind Mauna Kahālāwai. The day was ending, but at the same time it was the beginning for Hoʻāla and Naupaka.

AFTERWARD

Uncle Kawaiola's Dream: A Hawaiian Story may be thought of as a dream shared by only a few passionate, dedicated, and hard-working Hawaiians. But those who dream about restoring the 'āina and lo'i kalo, and then follow through by actually doing so, have made their dream more than just a passion or a pastime. They have made it their way of life.

This way of life is not without challenges. First, growing kalo requires hard work. Restoring stone walls for terraces, tilling the soil, building banks, developing an irrigation system, maintaining the 'auwai, weeding, controlling diseases and invasive species, and doing general maintenance will keep any kalo farmer busy. In addition, kalo farmers need to be able to perpetuate their way of life by following ancient Hawaiian farming practices and methods.

One can only imagine the Hawaiian way of life during the time of the Mahele of 1848. The quivering kalo leaves covered ahupua'a from mauka to makai, such as from Waikapū to Waihe'e on Maui. The view of these terraced lo'i must have been spectacular. Equally impressive must have been the resonating sounds of hundreds of pōhaku ku'i 'ai as Hawaiians made pa'i 'ai for poi to feed and nourish their 'ohana.

Today, with the decline of large-scale agriculture, Hawaiians are restoring long-fallowed lo'i and bringing life back to their 'āina. At the same time, they are working diligently to restore stream flow for Nā Wai 'Ehā—the four Central Maui streams of Waikapū, Wailuku, Waiehu, and Waihe'e—as well as the many other streams in East and West Maui.

Hawaiians who are returning to their 'āina to grow kalo know, as did their ancestors, how important kalo is. Kalo has been the staple food of Hawaiians for centuries. More important, though, is its cultural significance. The story of Hāloa tells how kalo is both the "elder brother" of the Hawaiian people and the "root of life" providing them sustenance.

For Uncle Kawaiola, the main character in the story, it was important to dream, but more important that he try to turn his dream into reality. His dream, which was rooted in passion, could have been short-lived. Instead, however, he used his passion as a springboard to something greater. Uncle Kawaiola's passion became his way of life. His dream to restore lo'i, once fulfilled, allowed him and his 'ohana to reconnect with the 'āina and each other.

I hope that *Uncle Kawaiola's Dream: A Hawaiian Story* inspires readers to follow their dreams. Whether pursuing a new dream or reclaiming an old one, I hope the story helps readers to build, to nurture, and to perpetuate their own way of life just as Uncle Kawaiola did.

Victor C. Pellegrino
Waikapū, Maui, Hawai'i
2010

A STUDY GUIDE FOR UNDERSTANDING AND LEARNING

1. Everyone has a dream story to tell. What is yours? Write about it and explain how you can make it come true. Draw pictures to illustrate your story.

2. Why do you think Uncle Kawaiola especially liked telling the story of his dream to children?

3. Why do you think Uncle Kawaiola's dream story inspired many who heard it?

4. Why did Uncle Kawaiola explain the meaning of 'ohana to the children? Draw a picture of a kalo plant and its 'ohā. Label the leaf, the stem, the 'ohā, the corm, and the roots.

5. Why is it important to dream about achieving something? Who helped Uncle Kawaiola achieve his dream?

6. Why is it that Naupaka is confused about sleeping dreams and waking dreams? Do you think she understood the difference by the end of the story?

7. Is Uncle Kawaiola's dream more about reclaiming the 'āina, bringing back Hawaiian culture, or both? Explain.

8. Why did Uncle Kawaiola ask his parents to plant the huli first, his 'ohana to plant next, and wait to plant his last?

9. There are several important symbols in the story. Find information that will help you understand the importance of the Hawaiian culture by using the following words: pule, 'aumakua, rain, and 'ohana.

10. How does the Hawaiian saying, 'A'ohe hana nui ke alu 'ia (No task is too big when done together by all) fit into the story of *Uncle Kawaiola's Dream*? Why do you think Uncle Kawaiola's father was so unwilling at first to understand his son's dream? Does our modern way of life separate people or bring them together? Why is it that friends, family, and kalo farmers came together to help Uncle Kawaiola? How can we make changes so families and friends stay in touch and help each other more?

11. Passion, support, and hard work have something to do with achieving goals. Explain why.

12. Why do you think the author chose Uncle Kawaiola, Naupaka, Ho'āla, and Kalima as names for his characters? Are they just Hawaiian names, or do they contribute to the meaning and understanding of the story?

13. Look at each painting in the story. Explain how the artist captured the words and ideas of the author in her paintings. What ideas in the story does she emphasize the most in each painting? Why? What would the story be like without her paintings?

14. Visit a kalo farm with kīpapa stone walls that separate each lo'i. Using some small stones ('ili'ili) and some earth, build a small kīpapa wall. Angle it 22 degrees inward from bottom to top. Why do you think Hawaiians built these walls at an angle? How do you think they built the terraces and walls without modern-day tools?

15. Many problems face kalo farmers today. One is the lack of water. In the Hawaiian language, wai means water and waiwai means wealth. Explain the relationship between these two terms. How did Hawaiians use and share water resources? Do you think the decline of kalo cultivation affected Hawaiians' health and diet?

16. Read and study about the sugar cane industry in Hawai'i—its rise, decline, and practice of diverting water. How much water is needed to grow one acre of sugar cane? Although the sugar industry provided jobs, in what ways was the sugar industry harmful? Why do you think sugar companies took the water from Hawaiians who needed it to grow kalo? Is it fair for one farmer to take water from another farmer?

17. Who are Hāloa and Kāne? What is their importance to Hawaiians, especially in regard to cultivating kalo?

18. Find sayings in *'Olelo No'eau: Hawaiian Proverbs and Poetical Sayings* by Mary Kawena Pukui that are about kalo. Explain their meanings and importance to Hawaiians in the past, present, and future.

19. Contact several kalo growers. They are always willing to supply huli and teach you how to plant them and take care of them. Use pots or raised beds for cultivating dryland kalo. As a guide, refer to *Taro: Mauka to Makai*, 2nd edition, by UH-CTAHR-OCS.

20. Review the words and definitions in the glossary. Then find other Hawaiian words that have to do with cultivating kalo. Use the internet site http://www.wehewehe.org/ or use the *Hawaiian Dictionary: Hawaiian-English, English-Hawaiian* by Mary Kawena Pukui and Samuel H. Elbert. Ask your parents or teacher to suggest some words.

GLOSSARY

'āina .... land, earth

ahupua'a .... land division usually extending from the mountain to the sea

'aumakua .... family or personal god; ancestors who take on the shape of animals or plants

'auwai .... ditch or canal used to transport water from streams to lo'i kalo

Hāloa .... son of Wākea, father sky god, and mother Ho'ohokukalani; younger brother of Hāloanakalaukpalili, who was stillborn and became the first kalo plant; Hāloa is the ancestor of the Hawaiian people

hau .... Polynesian-introduced tree with small yellow flowers and intertwining branches that form thickets; planted as windbreaks; inner bark is used for cordage

hō .... Hawaiian expression similar to "wow" in English

ho'āla .... to waken; to rise up (character name: Ho'āla)

huli .... kalo plant cutting used for replanting

'ili'ili .... small, flat pebble or stone

ka lima .... the helper; hand (character name: Kalima)

kalo .... root crop which is the staple of the Hawaiian diet; the root is cooked and pounded into poi; the stem and heart-shaped leaf of the plant are also eaten; once more than 300 varieties existed; today there are about 84 varieties; the Polynesian derivative of kalo is taro

Kāne .... one of the four great Hawaiian gods; god of procreation, fresh water, and sea

kauila .... endangered endemic native dry forest tree; its hardwood was used to make the 'ō'ō

ka wai ola .... life-giving waters (character name: Kawaiola)

kīpapa .... Hawaiian style of terraced "dry stack" stone walls that are built at an angle and without mortar

koa haole .... invasive non-native tree from tropical America with small white flowers and brown seed pods

kōkua .... help

kukui .... Polynesian-introduced tree; also called candlenut because the nuts were used for candles; known as a symbol of enlightenment

kuleana .... responsibility

kūpuna .... ancestors; grandparents, relatives; elders; source of traditional cultural beliefs, practices, and values

laulima .... group of people working together

lehua .... variety of kalo that makes a purple poi

lo'i .... irrigated terrace or pond used to grow kalo lūʻau .... kalo leaf which is cooked and eaten

mahalo .... thanks, gratitude

Māhele of 1848 .... event which divided Hawaiʻi's lands amongst the king, chiefs, and konohiki (head of land division called an ahupuaʻa)

mālama .... take care of, preserve, protect

mana ʻeleʻele .... variety of kalo with a black stem and red piko

Maui .... name of one of the Hawaiian islands

mauka to makai .... from the mountain to the sea

Mauna Kahālāwai .... West Maui Mountains; mountain range running from north to south, encompassing many streams

moano ʻulaʻula .... variety of kalo with a pale red stem and purple piko

Nahau .... old family name

naupaka .... native shrub found in both the mountains and the sea coasts; it bears a half white flower (character name: Naupaka)

Nā Wai ʻEhā .... largest kalo-growing region in Hawaiʻi at the time of the Māhele of 1848; poetic name of the four great streams of West Maui—Waikapū, Wailuku, Waiehu, and Waiheʻe

Oʻahu .... name of the most populous Hawaiian island and the location of Honolulu, the capital of Hawaiʻi

ʻohā .... offshoots of parent kalo plant

ʻohana .... family, relative, or extended family

ʻōʻō .... digging stick or pole used to loosen soil to plant huli

paʻi ʻai .... hard, pounded but undiluted kalo; consistency is paʻa (firm, solid)

piko kea .... a variety of kalo with a light green stem and a white piko

piko .... place where stem is attached to the leaf of kalo

pōhaku kuʻi ʻai .... poi pounder

poi .... staple food of Hawaiians made from cooked kalo, then pounded and mixed with water

pueo .... Hawaiian short-eared owl regarded as a benevolent ʻaumakua

pule .... prayer asking for special grace or blessing

Waikapū .... first of four ahupuaʻa in Nā Wai ʻEhā, which is located at the base of the West Maui Mountains; the name of a town and stream on Maui

wai .... water

waiwai .... value, worth, rich

ABOUT THE AUTHOR

Victor C. Pellegrino, *Professor Emeritus*, taught writing and Eastern and Western literature at Maui Community College. He served eight years as chair of the Language Arts Division. He also taught courses in advanced writing and American literature for the University of Hawai'i.

Pellegrino was the first recipient of the Excellence in English Teaching Award presented by the Hawai'i affiliate of the National Council of Teachers of English. He also received the Excellence in Teaching English Award from the Hawai'i Branch of the English-Speaking Union of the United States. Pellegrino served on the editorial board of *Makali'i, The Journal of the University of Hawai'i Community Colleges*.

Pellegrino's books have guided writers for more than two decades. His WRITER'S GUIDE SERIES —*A Writer's Guide to Transitional Words and Expressions*, *A Writer's Guide to Using Eight Methods of Transition*, *A Writer's Guide to Powerful Paragraphs*, and *A Writer's Guide to Perfect Punctuation*—have been used by students, teachers, and writers in the United States and abroad.

Pellegrino's writing is not limited to the world of English. Pellegrino has written two reflective books: *Maui Art Thoughts: Expressions and Visions*, and *A Slip of Bamboo: A Collection of Haiku from Maui*. He has also published an Italian cookbook, *Simply Bruschetta: Garlic Toast the Italian Way*. As a cookbook author, Pellegrino has appeared on television shows in Hawai'i and on the Mainland. He has held numerous food demonstrations, taught many cooking classes, and conducted cookbook writing workshops. His most recent book, *A Journey into the Self*, is a collection of poems he wrote between 1956 and 2009. He recently completed two family genealogy books and is currently writing a novel and a vegetable-based Italian cookbook.

In addition to his own writing, Pellegrino has edited and assisted in the publication of numerous books for other authors from Hawai'i and the Mainland. He has been a presenter at several writing conferences, the most recent for the Excellence in Writing Institute. He has conducted self-publishing seminars for the Maui Community College Department of Continuing Education and for the Hawai'i Writer's Conference.

Pellegrino received his B.S. and M.S. degrees from the State University of New York, College at Buffalo. He has studied and traveled extensively in Japan, China, and Italy. In 1984, he was a Fulbright Scholar in India. He is married to Wallette Garcia of Wailuku, Maui. They have three children, La'ela'eokalā, Mahinamālamalama, and Hōkūao, and two grandchildren, Kamehanaokalā and Ka'imi.

Most recently, Pellegrino has become a kalo farmer in Waikapū. Restoring the ancient kalo terraces, lo'i, and 'auwai (more than 400 years old) with his family, neighbors, and friends was the inspiration for *Uncle Kawaiola's Dream: A Hawaiian Story*.

ABOUT THE ARTIST

Linda Rowell Stevens was born in Utah. Her family moved to Connecticut and then to Virginia where she attended college at Virginia Commonwealth University. After college, she took a trip across the country with Beeb Balzer, her best friend. She moved to Hawai'i in 1972 at the age of 21. In 1978, her son Nahele Kanoa Hillery was born. She married her second husband, Larry E. Stevens in 1987. Their home is in the beautiful rainforest of Pāhoa on the Big Island of Hawai'i.

For many years, Rowell Stevens was an award-winning doll artist. Her dolls were shown with the Leo Moss Society and displayed at the William Grant Still Museum in Los Angeles. Among her more important dolls were meticulous representations of King David Kalākaua, Princess Ka'iulani, and Queen Lili'uokalani—all now in private collections. She has been a participant in several Hawai'i art exhibitions and was awarded first place for one of her early paintings. She was a long-standing member of the Pacific Handcrafters Guild, and her work was included in Hawai'i Craftsmen displays. Her diverse talents include painting, sculpture, fashion design, jewelry, ceramics, and glass, which have been showcased in several one-woman shows.

Rowell Stevens' research for her doll representation of King David Kalākaua increased her love and respect for him and drew her to read his book, *The Legends and Myths of Hawai'i*. After reading the book, she shifted her focus to painting methods and techniques used by the masters to give her artwork the results she desired. She is now recognized for her reverential paintings of Hawaiian themes as well as for her exceptional artistic ability to portray Hawaiian people and Hawaiian scenes. Rowell Stevens worked on the oil paintings featured in *Uncle Kawaiola's Dream: A Hawaiian Story* for more than a year. It is her first book as artist-illustrator.

"When was it your turn to plant?" asked Naupaka.

"Next. I remember it so well." Uncle Kawaiola became silent again. "My 'ō'ō pierced the surface of the water and opened the earth below to receive my very first huli. I reached down into the water and planted it. To hold it in place, I piled some of the rich, muddy earth around it.

"At that very moment, I thought I heard the voice of great grandfather Nahau whispering, 'After many, many years, you have returned the kalo to the 'āina. Mahalo.' Or...was it the sound of rustling leaves from the old kukui tree nearby?"

For a moment, Naupaka and Ho'āla seemed to be daydreaming. They imagined Uncle Kawaiola standing tall in the sun, his long shadow cast onto the surface of the lo'i. They saw his first huli, firmly planted in the soil. Its leafless stems reached above the blue sky reflected in the lo'i. Everyone was excited to see this moment. They also saw Kalima standing on the banks of the lo'i. He was happy too. He knew that today Kawaiola had taken the biggest step of his dream. Then Uncle Kawaiola broke the silence, and their daydreaming ended.

"Well, I can tell you this. My father never doubted me again. In fact, everyone who helped bring the lo'i back to life was proud that our 'ohana had the vision to mālama the 'āina. Over and over, they expressed how happy they were to have been part of my dream, and even happier to have helped it come true."

But there was still much work to be done. Many more lo'i were waiting to be restored. And they would need more water from the stream too. The final chapter of Uncle Kawaiola's dream was still a long, long time away. Uncle Kawaiola remembered Kalima's words: "Dream it, Kawaiola. Let the Hawaiian in you dream it—but in small steps."

DIRECT PAYMENTS AND PERSONAL BUDGETS

Putting personalisation into practice

Jon Glasby and Rosemary Littlechild

Revised and substantially updated second edition

This edition published in Great Britain in 2009 by

The Policy Press
University of Bristol
Fourth Floor
Beacon House
Queen's Road
Bristol BS8 1QU
UK

Tel +44 (0)117 331 4054
Fax +44 (0)117 331 4093
e-mail tpp-info@bristol.ac.uk
www.policypress.org.uk

North American office:
The Policy Press
c/o International Specialized Books Services (ISBS)
920 NE 58th Avenue, Suite 300
Portland, OR 97213-3786, USA
Tel +1 503 287 3093
Fax +1 503 280 8832
e-mail info@isbs.com

British Library Cataloguing in Publication Data
A catalogue record for this book is available from the British Library.

Library of Congress Cataloging-in-Publication Data
A catalog record for this book has been requested.

ISBN 978 1 84742 317 7 paperback
ISBN 978 1 84742 318 4 hardcover

Cover design by Qube Design Associates, Bristol
Front cover image © Kevin Chettle. The image used on the front cover is from a painting
entitled 'Seeing the seaside which I never saw before', by Kevin Chettle.

The series of Kevin's paintings can be viewed at http://www.bild.org.uk/01kevin_chettle0.htm and
portray a moving account of his life from living in a long-stay institution to independence. Kevin now
lives in the community and earns his living through giving lectures and selling his paintings.

Printed and bound in Great Britain by Hobbs the Printers, Southampton